# In a P

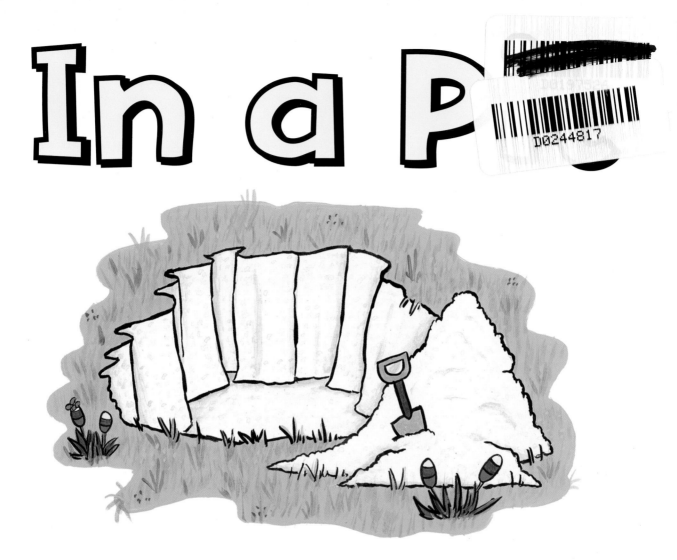

Written by Jane Clarke
Illustrated by Woody Fox

**Collins**

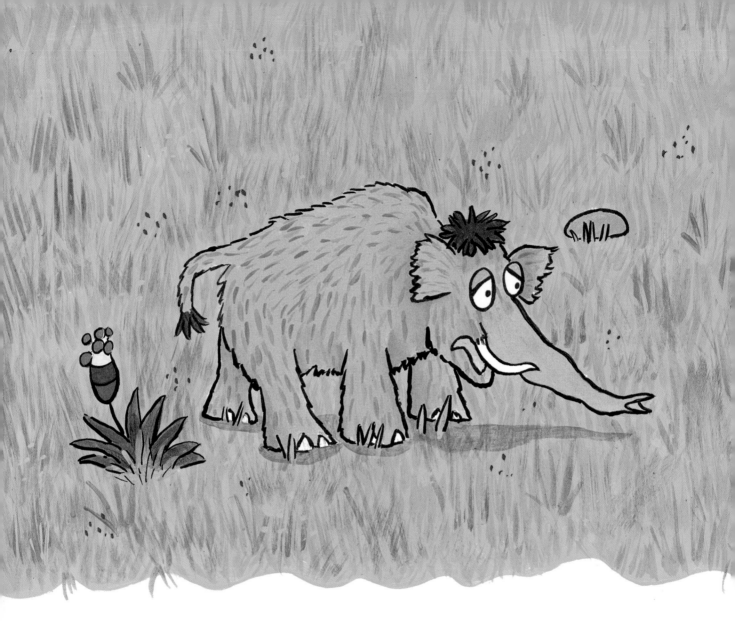

Sid is sad.

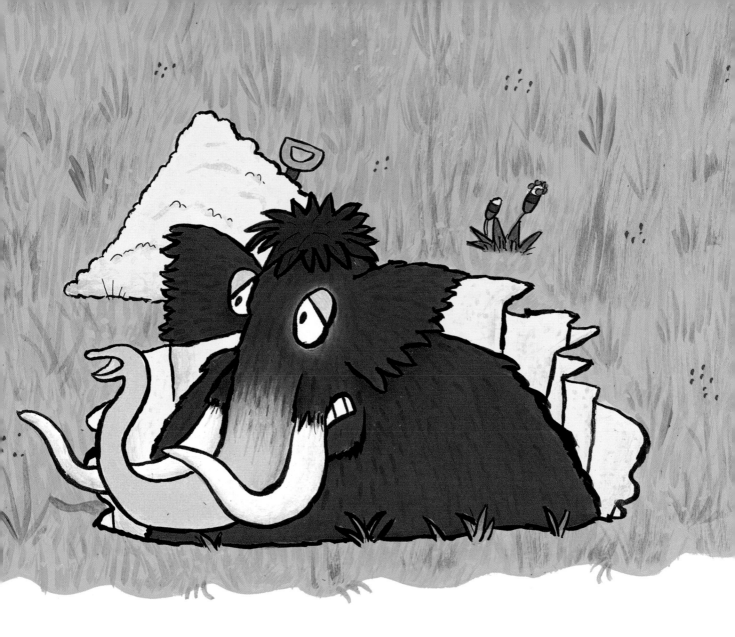

Dad is sad.

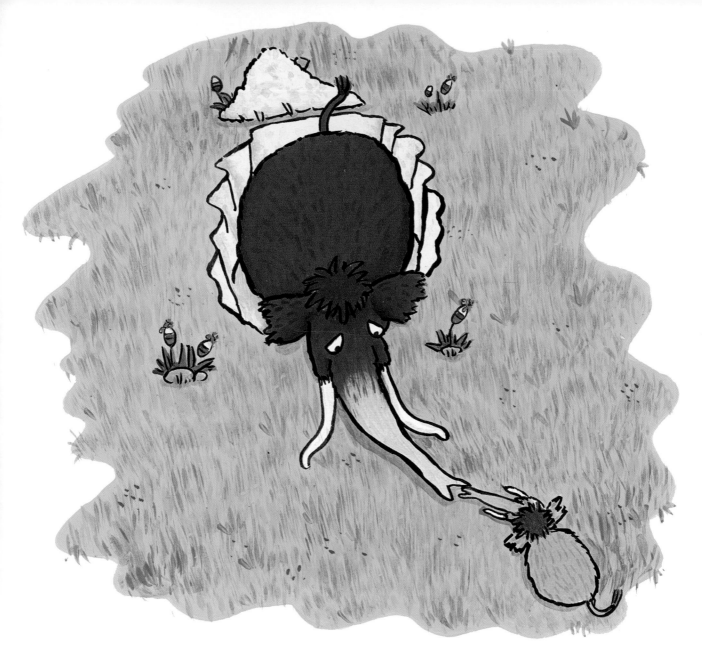

It is a pit.

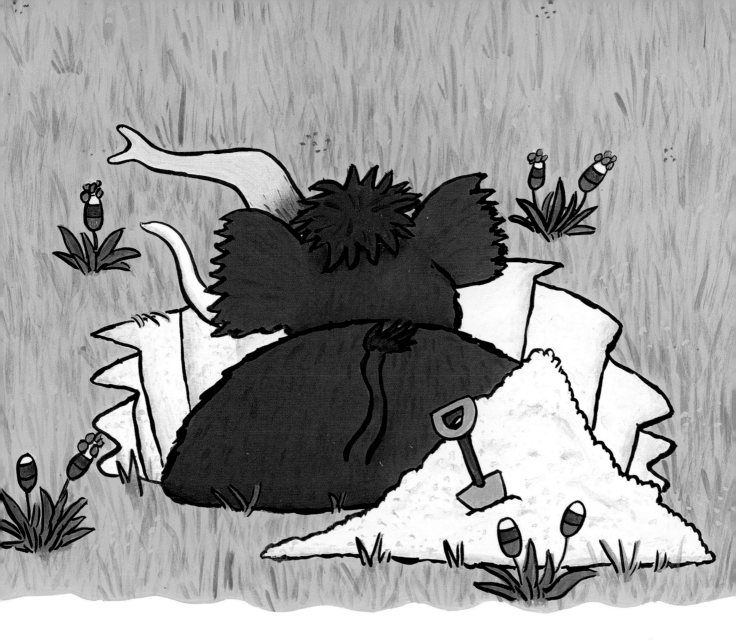

Dad is in a pit.

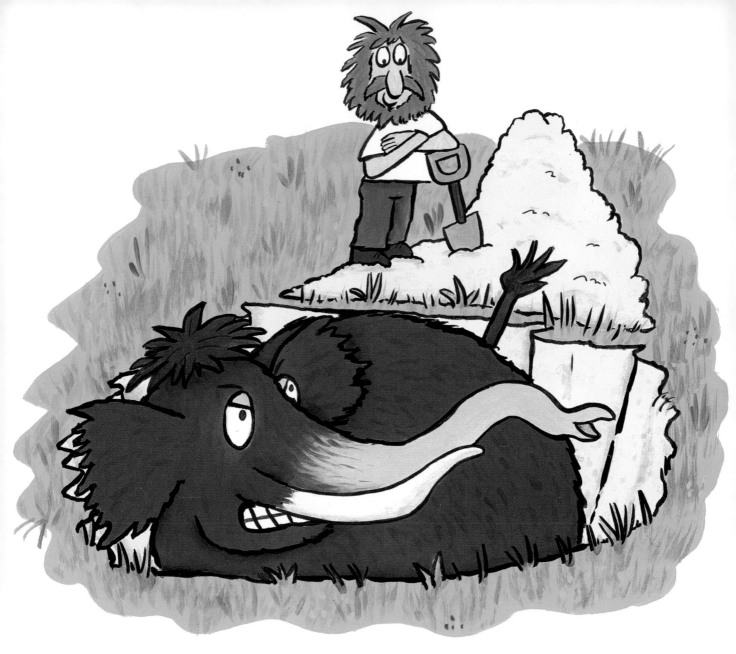

Man did it.

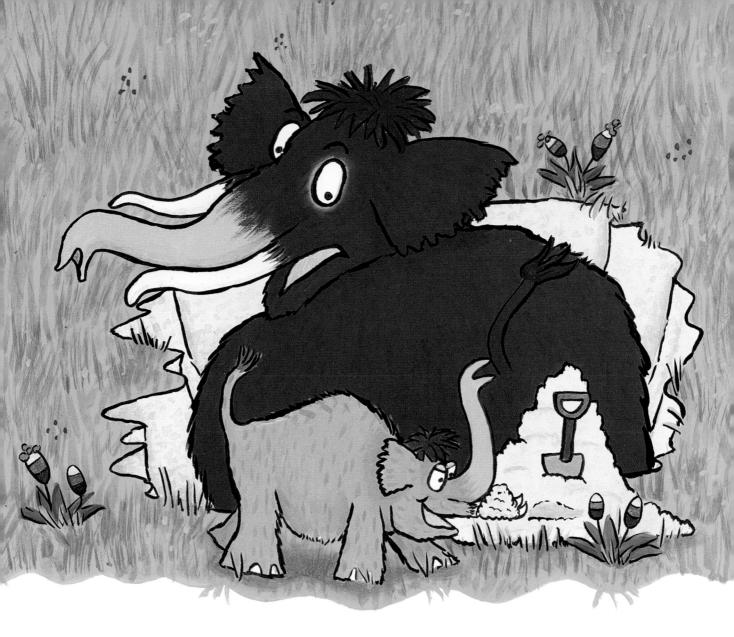

Tip it, Sid.

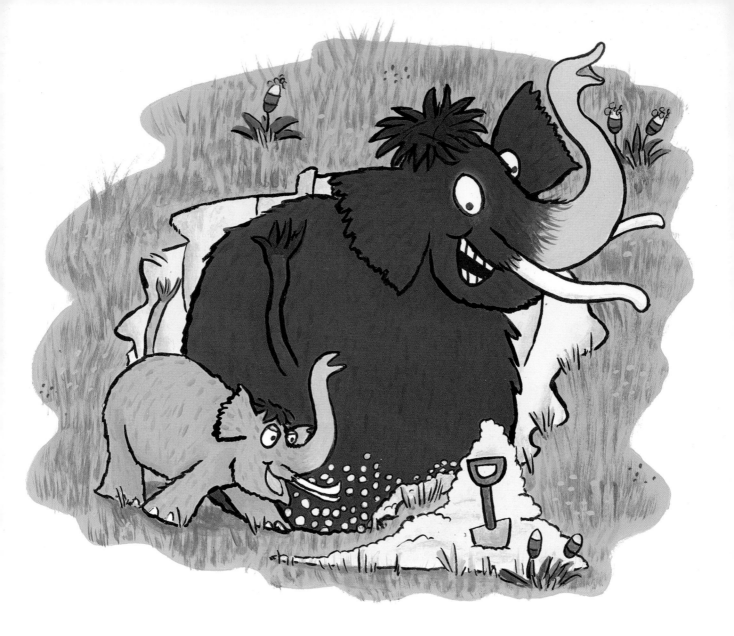

Tip it in.

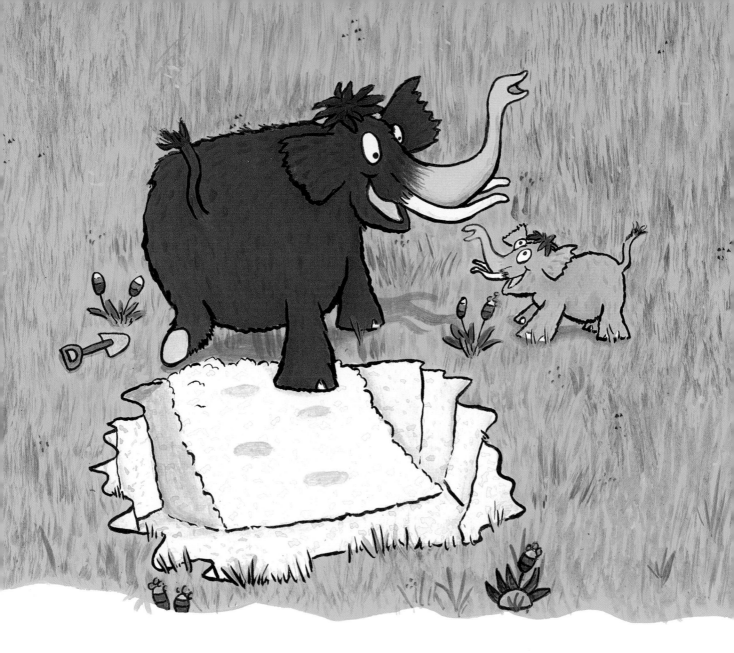

Sid did it!

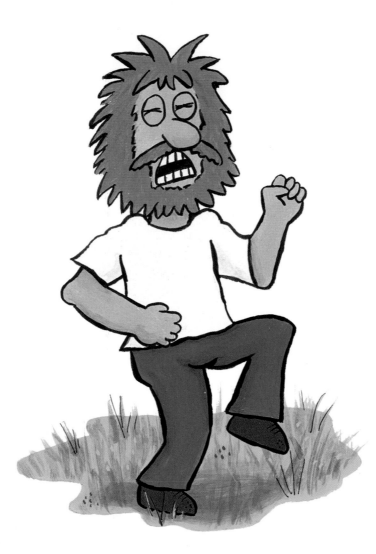

Man is mad.

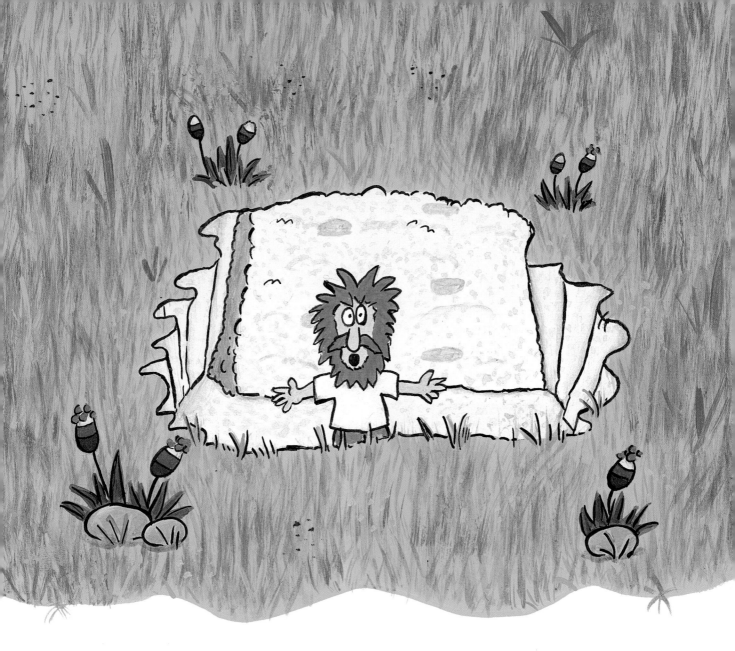

Man is in a pit.

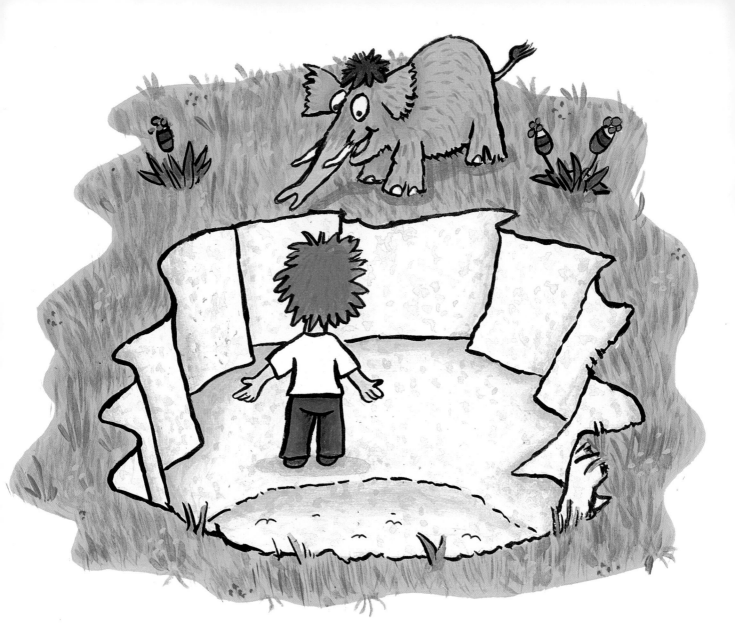

Did Sid tip Man in?

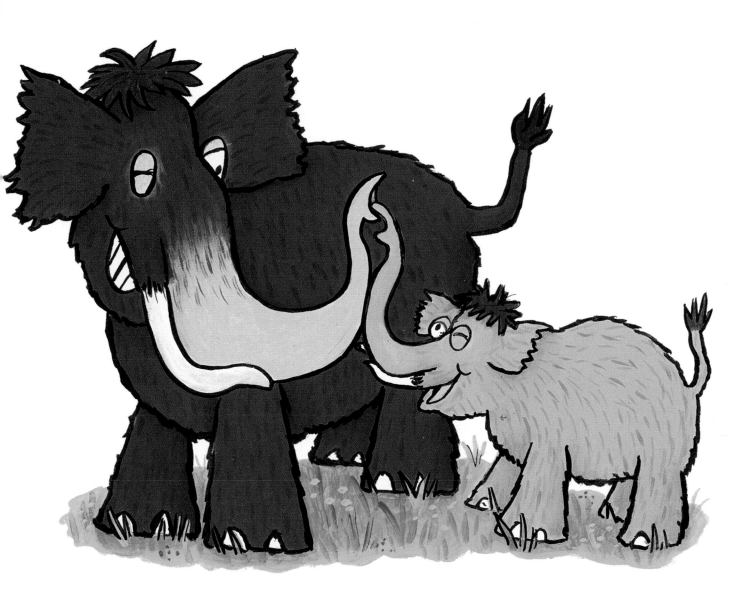

Sid and Dad did it!

# A story map

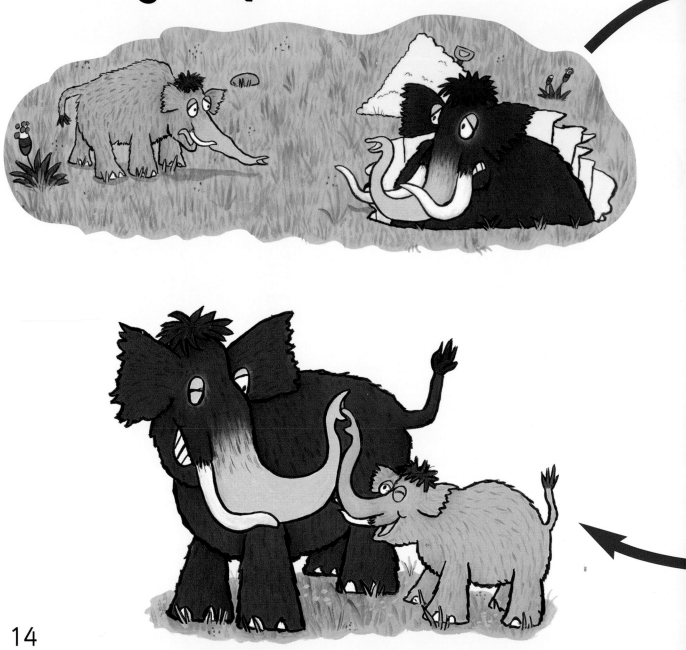

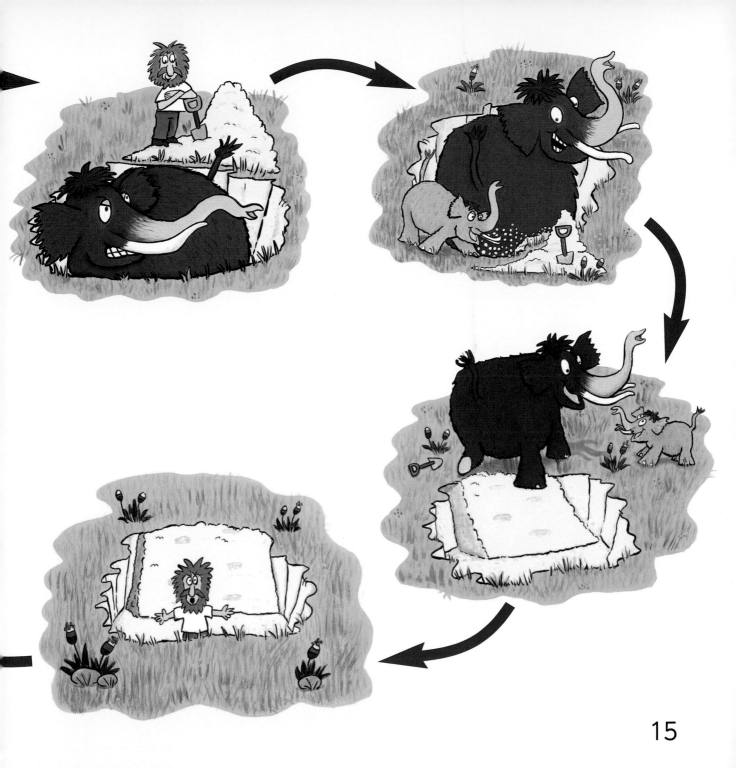